Pooh's Easter
Egg Hunt

DISNEY'S

A Winnie the Pooh First Reader

Pooh's Easter Egg Hunt

by Isabel Gaines

ILLUSTRATED BY Studio Orlando

SCHOLASTIC INC.

New York Toronto London Auckland Sydney
Mexico City New Delhi Hong Kong

ISBN 0-439-18694-3

12 11 10 9 8 7 6 5 4 3   0 1 2 3 4 5/0

Printed in the U.S.A.   24

First Scholastic printing, April 2000

Pooh's Easter
Egg Hunt

"Happy Easter!" Winnie the Pooh
called to his friends.

They were all at Rabbit's house

for his Easter egg hunt.

"All right, everybody," Rabbit said.

"Whoever finds the most eggs wins.

Get ready . . . get set . . . go!"

Pooh, Piglet, Roo, Tigger,

Eeyore, and Kanga

ran into the woods.

Pooh found a yellow egg

under some daffodils.

He put the egg in his basket.

Poor Pooh didn't know

his basket

had a hole in it.

The yellow egg slipped out

and fell onto the soft grass.

Piglet found the yellow egg.

"Lucky me!" he said.

Then Pooh found a purple egg

behind a rock.

He put the purple egg

in his basket.

Oops! This egg slipped out, too.

Roo found the purple egg.

"Oh, goody!" he cried.

"Purple's my favorite color!"

Pooh found a green egg in a tree,

and put it in his basket.

He didn't see it fall back out.

Tigger found the green egg.

"Hoo-hoo-hoo!" Tigger cried.

"I'm on my way to winning!"

Next Pooh found a red egg . . .

that slipped through the hole

and into a clump of thistle.

Eeyore found the red egg.

"Surprise," he mumbled.

"I found an Easter egg."

On the side of a grassy hill,

Pooh found a blue egg.

"How pretty."

Pooh continued up the hill—

as the egg rolled down it.

Kanga found Pooh's blue egg

lodged against a log.

Finally, Rabbit shouted, "Time's up!"

Everyone gathered around.

"Let's see who won," Rabbit said.

Piglet, Roo, Tigger, Eeyore,

and Kanga showed their Easter eggs.

Pooh looked inside his empty basket. "My eggs seem to be hiding again," he said.

Piglet looked at Pooh's basket.

"I think I know where," Piglet said,

poking his hand through the hole.

"You can have my yellow egg,"
said Piglet. "It was probably
your egg before it was mine."

"Thank you, Piglet," said Pooh.

"You can have my purple egg,

   too," said Roo.

"Here, Buddy Bear," said Tigger.

"Tiggers only like to win

fair and square."

"Too good to be true," muttered Eeyore,

giving Pooh his red egg.

"And here's my blue egg," Kanga said.

"You're the winner, Pooh!"

Rabbit said.

"You win an Easter feast."

"Is there enough food

for my friends

to eat, too?" Pooh asked.

"I could make more,"
Rabbit said.

"Is there enough honey?" asked Pooh.

"There's plenty of honey," said Rabbit.

"Then let's eat!" said Pooh.

Everyone had a wonderful time.

Pooh enjoyed the food—

especially the honey!

Can you match the words with the
pictures?

Kanga

basket

daffodil

purple

green

Fill in the missing letters.

P_oh

h_le

re_

_og

_oo